The House That Jack Built

McGRAW-HILL BOOK COMPANY

New York
Toronto
London
Sydney

THE HOUSE THAT JACK BUILT

Pictures by Paul Galdone

6200

This is the house that Jack built.

This is the Malt
That lay in the house that Jack built.

This is the Rat
That ate the malt,
That lay in the house that Jack built.

This is the Cat,
That killed the rat,
That ate the malt,
That lay in the house that Jack built.

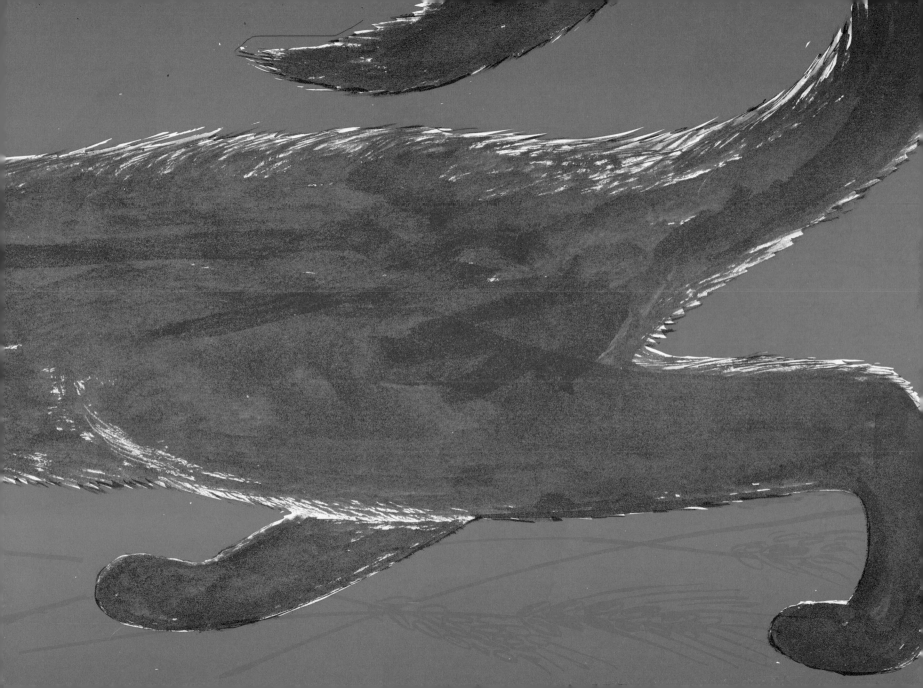

This is the Dog,
That worried the cat,
That killed the rat,
That ate the malt,
That lay in the house that Jack built.

This is the Cow with the crumpled horn,
That tossed the dog,
That worried the cat,
That killed the rat,
That ate the malt,
That lay in the house that Jack built.

This is the Maiden all forlorn,
That milked the cow with the crumpled horn,
That tossed the dog,
That worried the cat,
That killed the rat,
That ate the malt,
That lay in the house that Jack built.

This is the Man all tattered and torn,
That kissed the maiden all forlorn,
That milked the cow with the crumpled horn,
That tossed the dog, that worried the cat,
That killed the rat, that ate the malt,
That lay in the house that Jack built.

This is the Priest all shaven and shorn,
That married the man all tattered and torn,
That kissed the maiden all forlorn,
That milked the cow with the crumpled horn,
That tossed the dog, that worried the cat,
That killed the rat, that ate the malt,
That lay in the house that Jack built.

This is the Cock that crowed in the morn,

That waked the priest all shaven and shorn,
That married the man all tattered and torn,
That kissed the maiden all forlorn,
That milked the cow with the crumpled horn,
That tossed the dog, that worried the cat,
That killed the rat, that ate the malt,
That lay in the house that Jack built.

This is the Farmer that sowed the corn,
That fed the cock that crowed in the morn,

24

That waked the priest all shaven and shorn,

That married the man all tattered and torn,

That kissed the maiden all forlorn,

That milked the cow with the crumpled horn,

That tossed the dog,

That worried the cat,

That killed the rat, that ate the malt,

That lay in the house that Jack built.